The Magic Light

written and Illustrated
By
Noah carney

ONE NIGHT IT WAS DARK AND THE MOON WAS SHINNING AS BRIGHT AS IT CAN BE.

BUT SOMETHING HAPPENED THAT NIGHT. A TINY LIGHT BULB LANDED ON THAT VERY NIGHT.

ONE DAY

GOOD MORNING MOM!

MORNING, SWEETY. READY FOR BREAKFAST?

HEY ERNIE!

ARE YOU READY?

YEP.

BUT WHEN THEY WERE GOING TO SCHOOL, THEY FOUND SOMETHING RIGHT NEAR THEIR HOUSE.

WHAT IS THAT?!

I DONT KNOW.

THE MAGIC LIGHT

WHEN ERNIE AND DUCK PICKED UP THE LIGHT BULB, IT LOOKED LIKE A LIGHT. BUT NOT JUST A LIGHT BULB.
IT WAS A ... WELL, YOU KNOW...
IT WAS A MAGIC LIGHT.
HEY DUCK, YOU KNOW WHAT I SAW.

THE LENSES ARE A CONVEX LENSE BECAUSE THE RAYS OF LIGHT CAN PASS THROUGH TO FORM ANY IMAGE.

ARE YOU READY FOR THE JOURNEY TO VISIT KONG AND GODZILLA USING THE MAGIC LIGHT AND THEIR LENSES?

BUT WHEN THEY TOUCHED THAT LIGHT BULB OR SHOULD I SAY "MAGIC LIGHT" THEY WENT BACK IN TIME.
WHOH!
WHERE ARE WE?!
UMMMM?!
WHAT IS HAPPENING?!
IT LOOKS LIKE WE'RE BACK IN TIME! I TOLD YOU IT WAS MAGIC!
WOW!
WOW!
ROARR!
AHHH!
BAM!
BAM!
LET'S GO!
CAVE MEN!!!
OHAH GA!
OHAH GA!
AWWW-WWWW!
WE'RE GOING TO DIE!

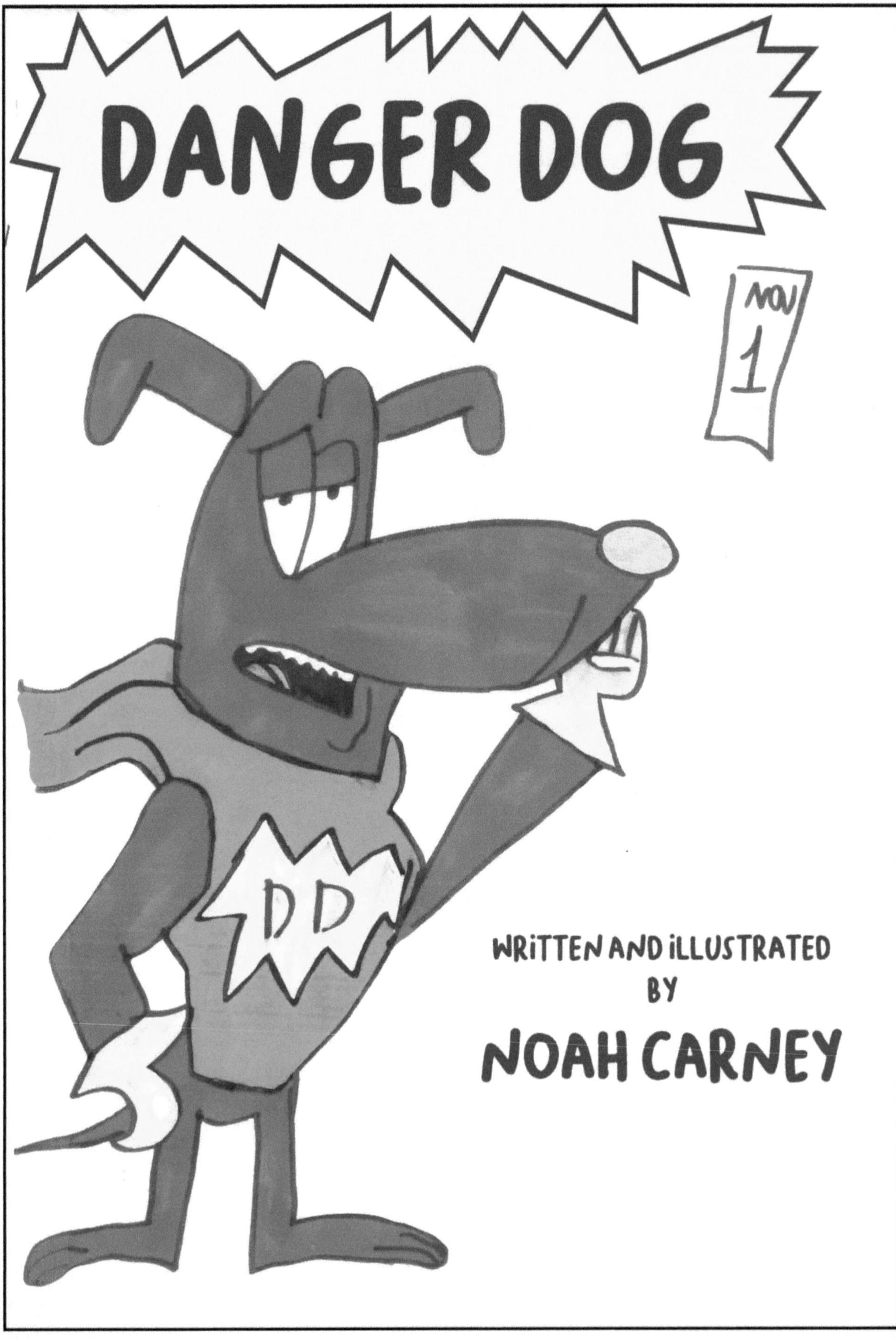
DANGER DOG
NOV
1
DD
WRITTEN AND ILLUSTRATED
BY
NOAH CARNEY

WHEN CAT-MAN WAS ABOUT TO DESTROY EVERYTHING, DANGER DOG SWAPPED IN AND CAT-MAN WAS BUSTED.

THE END

Pete THE Dragon

Noah Carney

THIS IS PETE AND HE IS A DRAGON.

PETE iS A COOL DRAGON.

PETE iS SMART AS A ELEPHANT.

PETE IS A FUNNY DRAGON.
HE ENJOYS MAKING PEOPLE LAUGH.

PETE IS SCARY LIKE A MONSTER.

PETE IS A NICE FRIEND AND DRAGON.

THE
END

THERE WAS A DOG WHO POOPED IN THE YARD ALL THE TIME.

THE DOG POOP IN THE YARD.

THE DOG POOP IN THE CITY.

THE DOG POOP ON THE ROBBER.

THE DOG POOPED IN THE NIGHT.

AND BACK TO THE YARD.